AF278795

To the Left of the Rising Light

Book II

by

William R. Underwood & Corvus

authorHOUSE®

AuthorHouse™
1663 Liberty Drive, Suite 200
Bloomington, IN 47403
www.authorhouse.com
Phone: 1-800-839-8640

First published by AuthorHouse 7/11/2008

ISBN: 978-1-4343-9252-7 (sc)

*Printed in the United States of America
Bloomington, Indiana*

This book is printed on acid-free paper.

Table of Contents

The Return

by

William R. Underwood

Gliding beneath the white clouds, a searching feathered predator was allowing himself to be carried by the high breezes. It was Hazard Hawk. He noticed a dark, feathered being disappear into a pine, near the lake, below him. Hazard had been watching that tree for many rising lights. He considered it part of his territory, and any creature near it, would be chased away.

He broke from the grip of the winds, and streaked toward that tree, and entered within its protective needles, ready to scold the intruder. Seeing the black, feathered trespasser, his slate gray plumage swelled. He angrily squawked, "Leave this place. It belongs to another!"

Startled by the furious sounds, the feathered stranger cautiously turned toward his possible opponent, recognized him, and quietly responded, "Hello Hazard."

When hearing the stranger, the hawk stood momentarily stunned. A better look allowed him to see whom he was facing.

"Corvus! You've returned! I wasn't sure if you were ever coming back. Are you here to stay?"

"Yes, Hazard, I am here to stay. This is my birth place."

"Good, good!" the hawk excitedly squawked. "You see that I have protected your favorite tree."

"Yes, thank you."

"Did your journey satisfy you?" inquired the hawk.

"Oh yes, Hazard. I managed to travel to the right of the Rising Light, three rising lights from here."

"What did you find, Corvus? the hawk questioned further.

"I came to a place that gave me shelter and a lighted perch from where I watched nonhumans and many humans. The area has plenty of light, and the cold times were a little shorter than here. There was no storyteller in that region, and since I did not wish to travel any farther from here, my birth place, so I decided to stay there and tell my stories."

"I am glad that your trek brought you contentment, Corvus," commented Hazard.

"It did," said the crow. "Anyhow, was this region fine without a storyteller?"

"I found another," responded the hawk.

"Oh," Corvus uttered.

"Everything is fine," Hazard reassured the storyteller. "Your replacement is temporary. I told him that I would try to help him find another region if you happened to return. He uses the cormorants' tree a short distance from here for his storytelling.

He has been a good help for the nonhumans of this area. But you, Corvus, are this region's only storyteller, now that you are back."

"Thank you again, Hazard, for your kindness toward me."

"That's OK. But now I will go and tell the other storyteller that I will help him find another place from which to tell his stories."

"Hazard, wait," Corvus interrupted. "I can save you some searching time. Have him come and see me. He can go to the region from which I have just returned. The place is now without a storyteller. There is no one there to tell the nonhumans stories. I will give him the route."

"Good idea, and Corvus, why don't you now use the cormorants' dead tree for your story telling. There is more light there, which, I am sure, you will appreciate, and you will be easily seen, plus, there are more perches for your audience."

"Sounds good, Hazard. This pine tree is little dark for me, but it is a good shelter. I'll do what I did three rising lights away. I'll have a place for a shelter, and a separate place for story telling."

"Again, Corvus, I am glad you have returned. I will go now and inform the other crow. By the way, I hope you don't mind sharing your new story telling place with cormorants."

"That will be fine," said Corvus.

The hawk then leaped from his piney perch, and headed for the cormorants' naked tree.

Corvus gazed pass the pine needles onto the lake. He was glad to be home.

Many raising lights later, Corvus was sitting at his new storytelling place, surrounded by the large, standing, feathered aquatic nonhumans. But he was also in the company of many small, safe, feathered listeners. He was ready to tell them a story.

Suddenly, the cormorants darted from their perches and raced to other parts of the lake. Corvus, knowing that these creatures were easily frightened, looked for the cause of their hastened flight. On the lake, and coming closer was a paddling human, yelling unknown sounds. As the human pushed nearer, the rest of Corvus's feathered listeners also took to the air. The storyteller stood alone in the naked tree. He focused harder on the approaching intruder. "How dare he interrupt my story," mumbled Corvus.

The rude human kept yelling his sounds. Corvus just stared at him. Somehow, the paddling, screaming, human stranger looked familiar. Was he the one from three rising lights away. How did he find me? Why did he find me?

The human quieted, and just drifted in his watercraft. For a few moments both beings simply stared at one another. Eventually, the human turned and began to paddle away. Corvus continued to watch, still puzzled. The paddler circled to face the storyteller one last time. Corvus, unable to answer his own questions, gently jumped from his limb, cawed a few good-byes, and winged for his pine shelter. He would tell his stories another day. The human turned his small craft again, and slowly paddled away from the cormorants' tree. He wondered if he had actually found Corvus.

A Crow among Cormorants

by

William R. Underwood

It had to be him. He was perched on a branch of a dead tree near the lake I was kayaking on. Sharing the limb with him were other, but smaller, safe, feathered nonhumans. From my distant viewpoint they could have been sparrows, wrens, or both. I couldn't tell. But I could recognize the larger, straight standing cormorants on the other naked parts of the lifeless tree.

If that was Corvus among those feathered nonhumans, he was certainly telling them a story.

As I paddled closer to what I assumed was his favorite tree, the cormorants took flight. The deceased tree seemed to give the old bird a good view of most of the lake, and there was plenty of light for him.

I knew the feathered storyteller wouldn't understand my sounds, yet I had so much to say to him. "Corvus! I've finally found you! I had only a rough idea where to find you! But after many days, I know now that I've found the right lake at the center of this northern island! It has to be you in that tree!"

Because of my excited and loud sounds, some of the smaller, feathered nonhumans also left their listening perches. I was interrupting a story, and, of course, a storyteller doesn't appreciate that. But at that moment, I disregarded my rudeness, and eagerly stroked toward the old tree to be beneath it. "Corvus! Do you remember me!" I realized that I was the one who named him. Yelling the sound of that name probably meant nothing to him. I still don't even know if nonhumans have proper names for humans, nonhumans, and all things around them. I suspect not. I continued to yell anyway. "I'm the human from the right of the rising light!"

The old bird cocked an annoying eye at me. My manners and sounds didn't seem to impress him. If he knew me, he didn't show it. He probably wished that I would had gone to a different part of the lake

I persisted. "Corvus! The region that was your temporary home is now without a storyteller. It has been awhile since one your stories has appeared in my thoughts!" Actually, I was never sure if Corvus had any control of placing stories in my mind .By the time I was under the tree, all of his feathered listeners were gone. He sat alone and high among those bare branches, eyeing the paddler below him. Minutes passed. Only the squawking sounds of distant gulls could be heard. The old bird continued watching me. Was this Corvus? I wasn't sure. I did know that I was tired. I had been on the lake for hours. It was time for me to leave. I've search enough in this region where I thought Corvus might be. Tomorrow I had to return to my home. For me, it was a journey of one day to the south. For Corvus, it had been a three day trek.

I began sliding away. After a few moments, I turned for one last look at the naked tree and the perching lone bird. He was still observing me. He then lifted from the deceased tree, turned away from me, sounded some caws, and vanished beyond the forest behind the tree. I too turned away, continuing to wonder if I had found the right bird Some weeks later, back at my home, during one of my jogs, I spotted a crow on what had been Corvus's favorite light pole. He was in the company of a few, small, safe, feathered nonhumans. I paused to observe the dark bird and his feathered companions. Had Corvus returned? I think not. He or she had to be a new storyteller to this region. Maybe Corvus understood me and sent another. Or perhaps, he had already known.

It is good to see another feathered storyteller on the light pole. I don't believe that he will have the same effect on me as Corvus did. Perhaps, I should give him a name too. Teller Crow should do.

Was it possible that during that brief eye to eye with that old bird, on that northern lake, that more stories might have entered my mind? I don't know. I resumed my jog.

Perilous Hawk

by

Corvus Crow

Corvus positioned himself on the naked limb of the lifeless tree, and, as usual, he was in the company of a few large, low grunting cormorants, who were scattered on the other bare branches. All had a good view of the rippling lake on this clear breezy morning, causing each feathered nonhuman to exert a little more effort to remain on its perch.

"Storyteller, why does your kind speak to the hawk? They are unsafe, you know."

The crow, startled, turned toward the quiet voice behind him. Nearby, on the same branch, was a motionless and stoic water bird. "What was that you said?"

"Why does your kind speak to the hawk?" repeated the cormorant.

"I thought most nonhumans knew why. Oh well, I guess not. Anyway, only crows like me talk to a certain breed of hawk.

They assign us regions, where we tell our stories. Hazard Hawk's father gave me this area."

"Oh," responded the cormorant.

"What is your name?" asked the crow.

"I am called Marinus," answered the water bird.

"I am called Corvus. This is my first time speaking to you, eventhough I have been perching here many times."

"I know," responded Marinus.

"Yes, I suppose you do," commented Corvus. "Well, I hope you don't mind me using this deceased tree for my story telling."

"We better let you use it, or we may have to answer to Hazard. But that's OK. The stories are fine. However, as we told the other story teller before you, the listeners have to be safe."

"I will tell my stories to unsafe nonhumans somewhere else," promised Corvus.

The large feathered nonhuman did not respond, but stood in silence, steadying himself against the wind while watching the choppy lake. Corvus would have to become accustomed to the hushness of these creatures. Anyway, the quiet is good for a storyteller.

"Corvus."

"Marinus, you speak again. What do you wish?"

"Why do certain hawks care for the story tellers?"

Back, long ago, not long after the time when many non-humans gradually began going into the night to live, and before nonhumans discovered how to speak outside their own kind, there were already crows who possessed the talent to remember all the stories they would hear, and with the ability retain all events they would see. But, unlike now, there was no special place for these dark feathered wonders to lecture. Each would convey stories from where ever he or she happened to be. Often then, in the same tree, there would be many storytelling crows, all chatting to other listening crows at the same time. Not only was it hard on those early listeners, the racket was even difficult for a storyteller. You would have thought that some of these black geniuses would have flown off to quieter areas. But no. There was too much pride in those birds. Instead, each would become louder, trying to outdo the other. The cawing would be deafening. In the end, both the telling crows and the listening crows would be forced to scatter to peaceful places of refuge, to recover from those unbearable sounds. The retreat was only temporary. The noisy cycle would repeat itself on the following day, and again, on the day after that, never ending. Of course, no one was happy, not only because of the crow clamor, but also, stories could not be completed. This was dissatisfying to the curiosity of the listener, and bad for the ego of the storyteller. Strangely, only the Maker of Nature knows, why these dark, feathered nonhumans, then, allowed this problem to persist as long as it did. These were dismal times for tellers and listeners.

The day came when this racket was also noticed by a feathered air predator. It was Perilous Hawk, a distant ancestor of Hazard Hawk. Seeing an opportunity to snatch some easy crow prey, the grayish hunter of the skies glided and skimmed across the tops of the trees toward the cawing uproar.

Undetected, he found a high spot in the same noisy tree, which enabled him to look down on all the ruckus. Perilous carefully began to eye one particular storyteller as a potential victim. Even though the "eye to eye" idea had yet to be discovered and understood by another, it has always existed unknowingly among nonhumans. Remember, for nonhumans of a different kind to speak to one another, we need to be eye to eye to interpret the other's sounds. With his keen hearing and sight to zero in on his selected prey, the hawk found himself listening to his target's story, not knowing why he was able to understand the teller's sounds. The crow's story began to hold his interest, and he forgot his original purpose for being in that turbulent tree.

But the dark, feathered nonhumans did not have the hawk's sharp and focusing ears. Again, unable to concentrate on any of the stories being told because of all the noise, one by one, the black, feathered listeners began to leave, to find quieter places.

The storytellers stopped telling their stories and quieted down. As they looked around for other listeners, in the highest part of the tree, the hawk was seen. Cawing out warnings to one another, the tellers winged away in all directions, including the one he had selected, disappearing into the surrounding forest.

"Wait! stop! you!" squawked the hawk. "Tell me the ending to the story!" Now alone, the hawk thought. "I must know the ending. I will find that dark bird so he can finish it for me." .Perilous leaped from his perch to search the sky and forest for that one storyteller. Many rising lights came and went for the searching hawk. He would often see several yelling storytellers together in a tree, but not the particular crow he was looking for.

Only the Maker knew how he would recognize him. Persistence pays. The hawk eventually spotted the dark storyteller. As usual, he was in a tree in the company of other screaming tellers. Gracefully and silently, Perilous found another tree in the vicinity which to hide, to watch, and to plan. From his present position, he would dart as close as possible, and then lunge, grab, and hold his black, feathered objective.

That is exactly what happened. As the other cawing crows dispersed, the captured crow looked up at the hawk and loudly begged, "Please, can you and I make a deal!?"

The hawk looked down at his captive. "What kind of deal?"

"Yipes! You understand me! OK, good. Release me, and I will tell you a story." Neither feathered nonhuman recognized the "eye to eye" idea.

"Oh, I understand you, and I already know what I want you to do, crow. You must finish telling the story you started some rising lights ago," demanded Perilous.

"What story! I tell many stories!" screamed the crow.

In another tree, I arrived and sat near its top. No one knew I was there listening. Eventually, because of the noise of too many story tellers, the listeners left, leaving only you and the other tellers," said the hawk. "That's when you saw me. You took flight, leaving me there, not knowing the ending to your story."

"You're right. We never saw you near the top of that tree. I do remember the story I was telling," said the crow.

"Good, now can you please complete it for me!" insisted the hawk.

"Only if you let me go," pleaded the teller.

"I can do that. But if you attempt to escape, I will follow until I find you," warned Perilous.

"I know," uttered the dark prisoner.

"You are free. Now, proceed with the story," requested the hawk.

The crow resumed his former upright position on the branch. "Hawk, do you remember where I left off in the story."

"Yes," answered the unsafe, feathered nonhuman. It was when...wait, just wait."

"What's wrong, hawk?" inquired the crow.

"Listen, crow, do you hear anything?"

"Just some distant chirping," answered the crow.

"That's right, crow! Isn't it going to be nice to tell your story to me in silent surroundings?"

"Yeeesss, but, don't forget, you are present, and that's why there are no other tellers here to tell their stories at the same time as me," responded the dark, feathered teller. "But, it would be nice."

The hawk thought. "You know, crow, it sure puzzles me why you and the other tellers always seem to pick the same tree for story telling. Why don't all of you choose different and separate areas?"

"We have talked about that. But we can't agree on who should go to what tree. So we all wind up in the same tree again, yelling our stories to whomever is able to listen," answered the crow.

"Nobody is able to listen, but me, and that isn't easy!" squawked the hawk.

Shaken by the hawk's outburst, the crow steadied himself tighter on his perch, and meekly responded, "true."

Perilous continued. "For once, story teller, you listen. Since I enjoy the stories, I am going to find regions for the tellers, and assign each one of you, your own area from which to tell stories. Then I can listen in peace."

"But hawk, what if we are not pleased with the region you assign us?"

The unsafe, gray feathered nonhuman stood straighter and taller on the branch, humbling the trembling crow even more, and with a hawk's sharp glare, calmly answered, "I don't care if you don't like your assignment. All of you will tell your stories where I place you."

"Sounds good," answered the lowly crow.

"I am so glad that you agree," commented Perilous, as he relaxed himself into a more comfortable posture on the limb. "I am going to find those regions now. Tell your storytelling friends to be ready to find their own tree in those areas I select for them. I am sure all listeners will be happy with this region idea." The great bird then leaped skyward.

The crow cawed out to the hawk, "What about the story you wanted me to finish?!"

As he was gaining altitude, the gray feathered menace screeched back, "I'll be back, crow, I'll be back!"

The crow thankfully sat alone, relieved that he had been spared from the peril of the hawk. He wondered what region that clawed tyrant was going to give him. It was time to tell the others of the hawk's plan. The crow jumped from his limb, and vanished among the trees.

"As you see, Marinus," continued Corvus, "that hawk's descendants carried on with the region idea."

"Thank you for the story, Corvus."

"Anytime, anytime. It is what I do."

The large water bird again went silent to concentrate on holding his perched position on this clear, breezy day.

Corvus had had enough with the wind. He sprang from the his bare limb, and sailed across the lake's waves toward the protection of his pine needled shelter.

The First Storyteller

The sky was heavily clouded, and the air was seasonably cool. Leaves were randomly drifting to the forest floor, and to the rippling surface of the inland lake.

Sitting on his favorite branch, feathers fluffed against a chilly breeze, Corvus dreamingly gazed across the leaf-covered water. As usual, he was in the company of the sentinel-like cormorants, all perched on different parts of the dead, naked shoreline tree. One of them grunted. The storyteller turned toward the sound.

"Corvus, who was the first teller?" inquired one of the straight-standing nonhumans.

"What caused you to think about a first teller at this moment? Well, anyway, don't forget tellers are able to recall everything they see, and to remember everything they are told. This gift of gap from the Maker seems to be widespread among my kind. But, there may be tellers outside my kind too-I don't know. Back to your question. I am not sure if there was a first storyteller. Instead, many might have emerged at once as the need for tellers developed."

"We are not clear what you mean: 'the need for tellers developed,' grunted another.

"The cold times," continued Corvus, "only allows limited activity among nonhumans, and therefore, boredom is bred. Those among my kind with teller ability began telling stories, probably before many went into the night to live, to others of my kind in order to ease the monotony of the frozen period. After the discovery of the 'eye to eye,' stories could be told to nonhumans outside my kind."

"Thank you, Corvus," responded yet another cormorant.

Silence resume again. The teller turned back toward the lake. A cold puff of air ruffled his feathers. "The cormorants would soon be leaving again to their far- off winter home," he thought.

The Bear Who Couldn't Sleep

by

Corvus Crow

"Corvus! Corvus! Are you up there!"

The yelling and the cormorants suddenly taking flight, stirred the storyteller from a late morning doze on his favorite branch in the naked tree. "Who, what?" mumbled the bird as he slowly awoke.

"Corvus, it's too nice of a day to be sleeping. Wake up!"

"Yes, yes, you are right," answered the teller through half opened eyes. "Ruckus is that you?"

"It sure is!" answered the grinning raccoon, who was gripping the same branch as Corvus, but nearer the trunk.

"Ruckus, it's daylight. Aren't you suppose to be sleeping?"

"Corvus, you have forgotten. I have lost my night vision. I can only sleep at night, now, like you."

"True, true. But, why aren't you guarding your groups' sleeping place, like you usually do?" inquired the storyteller.

"Oh, they insist that I wonder and hunt first," answered the raccoon.

"Sounds fair," said Corvus. "I suppose you are up here wishing to hear a story."

"Well, yes," responded Ruckus.

"It's too bad that no one at night is a storyteller," commented Corvus. "Anyway, do you remember Whiff? You know, the bear in the story about Chat Crow."

"I remember the story," said the raccoon.

Long ago, soon after most learn to talk outside their own kind, and many had already gone into the night to live, there was whiff, a large, unsafe, furry nonhuman of the day. The cold times were coming, and his kind were preparing their winter sleeping places. His den was in the side of a hill that sloped to the edge of a lake. It was an area of mostly grasses and a few trees, so it was an easy view from his shelter to the water below. He snuggled himself inside facing the entrance so that he could see everything outside, including the lake, and wait for the coming of that long slumber his kind always experienced during the shivering period.

Light turned to dark, and back again, and again, and again. The darkness grew longer, and the light grew shorter. The sounds of the summer nonhumans became less and less. Snow began to fall and the lake began to become ice. The cold and dark times had arrived.

Through those passing days, Whiff must have tossed and turned, over and over, endlessly, because he could not sleep. He continuously watched events through his door, knowing that if he ventured out, he may not be able to find food. So, to conserve energy, he had to remain quiet in his sleeping place. Only the Maker of Nature knew why Whiff could not sleep.

One event that especially caught his eye was a wolf prancing to the center of the frozen lake below, gently picking up a lonely loon, and carrying him off somewhere. "Why was that crazy loon still here in the cold? If that wolf was Clement, the loon was lucky," the bear mumbled to himself.

Later, another, but more disturbing occurrence also got the bear's notice. Humans! Many of them! They were building barked, inverted "U" shaped shelters on the shore, blocking his view of the iced lake. It appeared to be the beginning of a permanent encampment. This was bad. He had lost his view of the lake! But even worse, if the humans knew of his existence above them, they would hunt him. Whiff was big and strong, but because of their great number, it would be hopeless to try to scare them off; and, also, because he had to conserve energy, it would not be wise for him to leave his sleeping place during the shivering period. Yet, something had to be done! This was his territory! He was here first!

For the remainder of the day he glared at the humans constructing their village. Night came, and he watched the human shadows before their fires. How could he rid this area of these humans?

As the Rising Light's numerous helpers became brighter in the night sky, a wolf began to howl. Whiff thought of Clement. Maybe, that furry, unsafe nonhuman could help him.

The following night, the wolf, being curious about the new inhabitants settling near the lake, strutted by Whiff's door.

"Clement!" whispered the bear.

The wolf hesitated in his own tracks. "Was that the gruffing sound of a bear?" thought Clement. "These are the cold times. Those unsafe nonhumans should be asleep!"

"Clement," Whiff whispered again.

The wolf turned. The sound did not seem to be threatening. Scouting the humans below would have to wait. He now wished to investigate the husky voice. Alert, and ready to dart away, Clement peered into the bear's den. The two nonhumans eyed one another in the semi-darkness.

"Whiff!" barked Clement. "Why aren't you asleep?"

"Don't be loud," answered the bear. "The humans will hear you."

"Ok, Whiff, but, why are you awake?" the wolf inquired again in a lower tone.

"I don't know. For some reason my eyes will not shut this chilly season. Anyhow, Clement, I need your help to rid this region of the humans near the lake below."

"Oh no, Whiff. There is not much I can do. Their number is too great."

"First hear my plan. I am sure you will approve, because I did see you carefully carry away a loon from the center of the frozen lake awhile ago. By the way, how is that feathered nonhuman?"

"The loon is fine," answered Clement wolf. "Don't tell anyone in my group. I have already been banned from them."

"I won't, unless..."

"Alright, I understand, Whiff. What is your plan?"

"I will need you and your group," requested the bear.

"Again, Whiff, I have been ejected from my group, because, at times, I show clemency, as I did with the loon."

"I believe that they wish to see the humans leave as I do," responded the bear. "The pack will listen to you."

"You might be right, Whiff. I'll try." After hearing the bear's scheme, the wolf turned from the cave's opening, and was gone.

As the Rising Light disappeared behind the horizon, a host of howls sounded from the bluffs above the human settlement. Whiff grinned in the darkness of his small cave. Night after night the wolves bellowed their sounds. Tiring of the noisy teasing from the wolves, the village sent some of its members to discourage the badgering. They would find no wolf. The humans tried ambush, but the clever nonhumans had scouts that informed them of such tactics. So, the wolf wailing continued, until one early, bright morning Whiff noticed that the lodges were finally coming down. The humans were leaving, no doubt to find another site. Where? The bear did not care, as long as it was not near his lake. His plan had worked.

"Whiff! Whiff! The humans have left! yelped Clement dashing toward the big nonhuman's sleeping place. The wolf looked into the bear's chamber. There, rolled into a huge furry ball was Whiff - sleeping. Not wishing to disturb this hairy giant, the wolf left.

High on a wintery, naked tree sat a crow named Chat. He had witnessed the cooperation between the bear and wolf. Whiff was a friend. Why had he been awake at this time? He took to the air to catch he wolf. Perhaps, he knew why.

"Of course, Ruckus, the humans have returned, and, now, in higher numbers," continued the storyteller. "It is Whiff, Clement, and their kind that have left long ago. But who would you harass if the humans were not here?"

The raccoon grinned when hearing Corvus's last comment. "I better leave. I have to return to my group's sleeping place to watch over them."

"Yes, you better," responded the teller.

The raccoon scampered down the naked tree and was gone. Corvus looked about the lake. Human made shelters now surrounded almost half of the lake. But with Ruckus gone, quiet had returned to the naked tree, and the cormorants began returning.

The Dam

by

Corvus Crow

The cormorants, looking like dark, straight sentries, sat in the naked tree, watching the lake. Among them, on his favorite branch, the black, feathered storyteller began his mid-morning doze.

His limb suddenly shook; his companions quickly jumped, and streaked across the lake.

Maintaining a tight grip, Corvus opened his eyes. Next to him was perched a large, unsafe, feathered, glaring eyed nonhuman. It was Elegant Eagle.

"Oh, ah, hello Elegant," said the drowsy crow.

"I see that my food competitors have fled," remarked the eagle.

"Do you blame them," commented Corvus.

"No, I don't," said Elegant as he straightened himself into a more imposing position on the branch.

"I suppose you wish to hear a story."

"I thought I would take a break from the sky and relax. Well, yes, please tell me a story," requested the eagle.

"I promised the cormorants not to tell stories to unsafe nonhumans here."

The eagle looked across the lake. "We'll go to my bluffs, there."

"Of course, your bluffs. Who would dare argue," mumbled the storyteller.

"Excuse me, Corvus, what did you say?"

"I said, of course, that sounds good!"

The feathered beings leaped from the limb, allowing the wind to lift them above the trees and to carry them to the distant cliffs.

Both landed together. From their rocky perches they could see most of the deciduous and evergreen trees that surrounded the lake, and the features of the land beyond. Corvus thought of a story.

The lake gave nourishment to all that lived near it, above it, and in it. So, the nonhumans of the area did not look favorably to the few humans who cut and cleared for food and shelter. The nonhumans also did not appreciate the lake's surroundings being turned into a land of stumps by one of its own - the beaver.

Regretfully, there was nothing that could be done about the regional destruction caused by the humans. However, a group gathering was called to resolve the beaver problem.

Fast moving dark clouds, fluttering, swishing leaves on bending trees, and rippling white caps on a restless lake, all created companions of the wind, were already present, as many nonhumans began to convene in a secret place.

With a firm grip on a shaking limb, Brazen Blue Jay shrieked, "Who called this meeting under these miserable conditions?"

"I am the one," came a voice from somewhere on the ground.

"Please, show yourself," insisted Brazen.

A small, slender, dark figure scampered up on a fallen tree trunk, stood on his two hind legs, and responded, "Here I am!" It was Mustela Ermine.

"Good, good," said Cagey Fox as he emerged from behind some shaking trees. "Now, why have you called this meeting? Hurry with your answer and speak loudly because the wind is noisy and ready to bring wetness.

"Yes, yes, you are right. I will try to be quick. It's the beaver," explained the ermine.

"What about the beaver?" Chirped many impatient voices from behind the waving leaves above.

"The beavers are cutting too many trees near the lake's shore. I need trees near the water for protection! yelled Mustela.

"Builder, Builder Beaver! Are you here! barked Cagey.

Many of the nonhumans both on the ground and in the trees looked around.

From among the crowd of nonhumans Builder Beaver emerged. He stood on his hind legs so all could see him better. "I am here."

The fox crept closer to him and said, "Mustela says that you are cutting too many shore trees. What can you tell us?"

"Builder! Builder!" Another beaver, yelling, suddenly dashed to the accused. "Our lake is in danger of losing its waters! The little human made dam is collapsing!"

The assemblage began looking at one another and commenting, "Without the dam, the lake would become too shallow!"

They looked toward the beavers, but the builders had quickly slipped away. Like a migrating herd, the group began making their way through the turbulent trees and underwood toward the dam at the far end of the lake.

The lake's surging fury was still pounding the small, damaged dam as the worried nonhumans began to arrive. Peering from behind trees and rocks, they saw that the beavers were already working to mend the breach in an attempt to stop the lake from bleeding heavily into the small stream beyond the little dam. However, as fast as the aquatic builders struggled in the rushing waters to plug the dam's opening with logs and sticks, the relentless current would drag the wood, and an occasional beaver, through the cut, sending them crashing somewhere downstream. Those persistent beavers would somehow pop out of the racing stream at the nearest bank, grab more wood, and drag it back to continue the repair. This beaver tenacity continued through the day in spite of the storm. Eventually, waves give way to the ripples, leaves became motionless with only dripping water, and spots of blue appeared between the clouds. With the calmness, the tired beavers had succeeded in their efforts. The lake had been saved. Humans would have to complete any final fixing. The region's nonhumans were relieved and thankful for the beaver's labor and courage.

The wet crew of beavers came up on the shore, shook the moisture off themselves, and sat to recover from their dam patching ordeal.

Cagey Fox approached them and said, "We who live in this area, thank you for saving our lake."

"You are welcome, but my kind especially need the lake," responded Builder Beaver.

"Wait! Wait! yelled Mustela Ermine. "What about the beavers cutting and gnawing so many shore trees!"

"Silence, Mustela!" barked Cagey. "Let me think." Only the sounds of dripping were heard from the surrounding foliage. But the quiet was quick. "Builder, we know your need to gnaw," continued the fox. "But, please cut less shore trees."

"Sure, Cagey, we'll chew fewer trees by choosing our favorites a little more further from the water," replied Builder.

"Good!" yelped the fox. He then looked at the ermine. "Mustela, are you satisfied?"

"Yes, I think so," muttered the unsure nonhuman

Satisfied with ermine's answer, the fox turned away, as did the others, and disappeared into the wetness of the woodlands. Without causing a single splash, each beaver returned to the lake, and were gone. Mustela stood alone. Eventually, he too scampered away to look for food among the shoreline rocks.

A crow flew from a high tree, leaped and landed on the pile of wooded debris that prevented the lake from shrinking. The black feathered nonhuman marveled at what the beavers had done to save the lake.

"See, Elegant, the lake below is still there. The beaver's wooden dam is gone, but a new little stone dam built by humans now keeps the lake level in place.

The eagle scanned the expanse of the lake. " Well, I must look for what lives in the lake." The great bird spread its wings, and was lifted by wind.

Corvus remained on the bluff to enjoy the view of the lake's expanse.

The Night Teller

by

Corvus Crow

"Corvus! Wake up! It's not night!

"Wha, wha. Who's sound? Oh, hello, Ruckus. I was just napping."

"Good morning, Corvus. A late morning to you," greeted the raccoon."

The crow stretched his wings, and looked around. As usual the cormorants had fled with Ruckus's arrival. The lake was calm, and the cloudless, summer day was pleasant. "Ruckus," cawed the storyteller, "shouldn't you be wandering at night? Wait. I forgot. You've lost your night vision."

"True," replied the raccoon, dishearteningly.

"Cheer up," said the storyteller. "Being in the Light allows you to come here to listen to my stories."

"True again, Corvus, but my group has told me that there is a Night Teller in this region.

"There is!" cawed the crow. "I have often thought that there should be a storyteller for the nonhumans who live in the night. But, that teller can't of my kind."

"I don't know," remarked the raccoon.

"Ruckus, do you know of anyone who has listened to night teller's stories?"

"No, I don't, Corvus."

"I am curious," uttered the crow. "I wish to find this night teller. It's too bad that your night vision is gone, Ruckus. You might have helped me hunt for this nightly storyteller. I would like to meet this nonhuman to see if it's feathered, furred, safe or unsafe."

"You will have to find another to aid you in the dark," said the raccoon.

"Let me think," mumbled the day teller. "I don't know many nonhumans of the night. But, there is one who is comfortable in the day and the night, and that would be Catus."

"Who is Catus?" questioned Ruckus.

"A cat who lives among the humans near here. Occasionally, he climbs up this dead tree to hear a story," answered Corvus. "His needs are met by the humans, so he won't be busy hunting; and, he has night vision."

"Do you think that feline will help you?" inquired the raccoon, again.

"He will, or no more stories for that furred nonhuman," responded Corvus. "Anyway, Ruckus, I will go now to ask Catus for his assistance. You come back in several Rising Lights, and I will then let you know if we was successful."

"OK, Corvus. I hope the Maker is also with you during your search."

"Thank you, Ruckus."

"Corvus! Corvus! Wake up! It's not night!"

"Wha, wha. Oh, hi, Ruckus. I was just napping."

"Corvus, you asked me to return after several Rising Lights. Well, I have. Did you find the Night Teller?"

"Yes," said the yawning, feathered storyteller, stretching his wings.

"That's wonderful! Tell me more! Was the Night Teller feathered, furred, safe or unsafe?"

"Ruckus, hold on. Give me a chance to awake completely. Then I'll tell you."

The large black teller looked around. Of course, the cormorants had been frightened away, again. The lake was a little choppy on this mild summer day. It was a good day to tell a story.

I found Catus where I thought I would find him. The cat was slumbering on a wooden extension of a human made shelter. Seeing no human presence in the area, I glided down to the sleeping nonhuman. My sudden arrival awoke the cat, and, thank the Maker, I was recognized immediately.

"Hello, Corvus. Welcome to my home. I have been waiting for you."

"You have! How did you know that I was coming?"

"The word moves quickly among nonhumans," answered Catus.

"So it does," commented the teller. "Then you also must know that I need your aid."

"Yes, but just to let you know that most of my wanderings are under the Rising Light."

"Why is that?" questioned the crow.

"Look at me, Corvus. I am the opposite of you. The Maker made me as white as snow! In the darkness, among the underwood, I'm easily seen. However, my night vision is fine. So, I will assist you as best as I can in looking for this Night Teller."

"Thank you, Catus."

Is this phantom teller feathered, furred, safe, or unsafe?" asked the cat.

"I was hoping you would know; but since you don't move about at night too much, I suppose you don't know," commented the day teller.

"If it is large and unsafe, we may not be welcomed in its dark world," said the concerned cat.

"Are you changing your mind about helping me?" inquired the crow.

"No, no. I am just being a cautious cat."

"I believe it's good to be careful," remarked the storyteller. "Anyhow, the Rising Light is lowering itself behind the trees. We should begin our journey. I'll ask nonhumans in the trees about this Night Teller. You ask those who dwell on the ground. We'll stay within hearing distance of one another. Be careful of unsafe nonhumans.

"I sure will. Somehow, I am convinced that this Night Teller knows we are coming," muttered the worried cat.

"Maybe so, Catus. Maybe so."

The two of us quietly made our own way through the dark trees, trying to ask any nonhuman where to find the Night Teller. But, to our misfortune, these shadowy forms that live beneath the dim light of the Light's Helper, were either frightened of us, or much too busy for us.

Tired, after many near misses when reaching for branches in the darkness, I carefully floated down to Catus.

"Did you learn anything, Corvus?" asked the cat.

"Regretfully, no. I am so awkward in this murky place. Even the eye to eye is hard here in this dimness. Nonhumans have to be very close to one another for it to work. That is why it so quiet, because there is little or no talk."

"I have been unsuccessful too. They see me before I see them. I only see them quickly flee," said the frustrated cat.

Crack! Crash!

Both of us, with eyes wide opened, stiffened with the sudden sound. After a moment of silence, we realized a dead tree had fallen nearby. The racket had worsened our fears of this hazy place.

"That's it! I've had it!" screamed the cat. "This Night Teller is just a rumor. It's too dark here to tell stories, besides having a storyteller. I am also tired. Let's go back, and forget about our search."

"Perhaps, you are right," agreed the crow.

As we turned toward the dim direction from which we had come, we heard another sound. It was not loud. Many nightly noises were familiar to us, but this one was new to us. We stood motionless, straining to listen for that sound. Again, the little sound was heard, but closer. It was a raspy call, yet not too harsh. Looking around in the gloom, the cat noticed a large vague figure, in a clearing, blocking our way home.

"Oh my, Corvus, what is it?" whispered the cat.

I too was staring wide eye at the murky form. "I don't know," I said, quietly.

Daringly, we decided to get a better view, being alert to take fast flight, in our own way, if the need came. Creeping closer, we were relieved to see that the shadowy shape was only a small feathery nonhuman atop a stump. It did not try to escape. I quickly leaped up beside it to talk. It was smaller than me, hooked beaked, and round headed. On both sides of its bill were big circular eyes, inside even larger facial discs. It was an owl without the usual ear tufts.

"Why haven't you taken flight like anyone else here?" I asked.

"Should I?" responded the owl.

"I have a cat with me. That's a good reason to cause you to flee."

"I suppose," said the night bird in a hoarse tone, but not moving anywhere.

Catus and I glanced at one another in bewilderment. I then decided to take advantage of this stationary nonhuman and asked, "Where can we find the Night Teller?"

The elfin owl blinked its great eyes, and replied, "That's easy."

I rudely interrupted. "You actually know! I was beginning to think that the Night Teller was a myth!"

"Please, please," continued the owl, calmly. "Let me finish."

"Oh, yes, excuse me, please do," I humbly said.

"This stump, in this clearing, is where the Night Teller waits for listeners. Come back when the Light's Helper is full faced. Only under its dull brightness will the eye to eye work well for us nightly nonhumans. It is only then stories can be told, unlike your daily stories, Corvus, under the bright brightness of the Rising Light."

"You know me. Wait, I know. The word moves quickly among nonhumans," commented the day teller. "Oh, excuse me, this is Catus. He has been aiding me in finding the Night Teller."

"Yes, I know that too," responded the owl. I am called Raspy."

"OK, Raspy. We will return here when the Helper's light is right. I hope the Night Teller is safe,"

"The teller is safe, Corvus." assured the owl.

We thanked the little, feathered nonhuman, and slowly found our way back to our sleeping places, anxious to return later when the Helper was at its most radiant.

Several Rising Lights later, Catus and I were again trekking through the filmy foliage. This time, with the help of the Helper, all shapes were more visible, making our journey simpler.

Finally, we reached the clearing, with the stump at its center. On it was someone. Hopefully, it was the Night Teller. We slowly advanced. To our surprise, it was Raspy sitting on the stump. I hurried to him.

"Raspy, where is the Night Teller?" I quickly asked.

"Hello, Corvus. You too, Catus. Do you wish to hear a story?" inquired the owl.

Puzzled, I cocked one eye at the smaller bird, and again requested. "Where is the Night Teller?" Again, the owl answered, "Do you wish to hear a story?"

I looked at Catus, who, by now, had its forepaws on the stump. I then gazed into the clearing and the blackness beyond. "Catus," I calmly said.

"Yes, Corvus. Is there something wrong?"

"No, no. Please, look about you."

The cat turned, and scanned the clearing. Many dim dots, nocturnal eyes reflecting the Helper's weak light, glistened in the surrounding blackness. All were patiently waiting.

Corvus continued. "Catus, it is my pleasure to introduce to you, the Night Teller."

"Where, Where?" inquired the cat, twisting about in all directions.

"Sitting beside me, Catus, sitting beside me," answered the Day Teller.

"Oh my," uttered the cat. "It's the little owl."

"I am sorry I didn't tell you earlier who I was, but I was just having fun with the two of you," said the Night Teller.

"No wonder you did not run from us. Tellers are protected by all," remarked Corvus.

"That is correct," answered Raspy.

"Are there more of you?" questioned the crow.

"Of course," replied the owl. "We have regions too, but we assign areas to ourselves, unlike you who use a hawk for that purpose. We are nocturnal loners who need no one to find us telling places. But, sadly again, my stories are given only under the Helpers full light, whereas, your stories are daily."

"I suppose many of your kind are tellers because of your ability to retain what you experience and hear," commented the crow.

"Yes," responded the owl.

"Cheer up, Raspy, telling your stories when the Helper is at its best causes you to gather a large group of listeners. We tellers like that."

The owl opened his eyes wide with pride. "Yes, Corvus, you are right!"

"Your listeners are waiting, Night Teller," said the Day Teller.

"Then, let's not have them wait any longer. Corvus, please tell us a story." begged the owl.

"Me. This is your domain, where you don't have much opportunity to tell stories, especially if the Helper is covered," reasoned the crow.

"Your visit is rarer," rebutted Raspy.

"You are right, teller. I don't come here often. OK! I would love to tell a story to this crowd," Corvus cawed excitedly standing proudly near the Night Teller on the stump.

"Now, Ruckus, you can tell your group who the Night Teller is, and where find that nightly storyteller."

"Thank you, Corvus. I sure will. They can now hear stories too."

The raccoon quickly scampered down the dead tree. With that furry nonhuman gone, the cormorants would return shortly. Meanwhile, another nap was due for Corvus. It had been a long night of story telling. As the crow's eyes gradually closed, he imagined other tellers, of other kinds, in more distant places.

Coming of the Cormorants

by

Corvus Crow

A sweeping chilly breeze disturbed the leaves and white capped lake. His eyes closed against the rushing air, Corvus tightened his grip on his favorite branch of the dead tree he shared with the cormorants.

They were gone for now. Only warm winds that would free the lake of its eventual ice would bring back all the water dependent, feathered nonhumans.

"Corvus. You are finally sitting alone on this bare tree."

The startled storyteller quickly spread his wings and hopped a wing length farther out on his limb. He had to tilt an eye up to see who had suddenly perched nearby. It was Elegant Eagle. "Yes, I am now alone here," responded the teller. "The quiet lake flyers and floaters have gone until after the frozen peroid."

"Good. At least, I'll have the lake for hunting to myself," commented the eagle.

"Until it freezes," mumbled the storyteller.

"What was that? I didn't hear you, Corvus.

"There are strong breezes."

"Yes, there are," agreed the eagle. "Anyway, as you will know, there was a time when I had less competition on this lake all through the warm period. There were no cormorants. Why did they come?"

The day teller squinted to look across the rippling lake into the direction of the Rising Light. Ordinarily, because of the shyness of the cormorants, he and an unsafe nonhuman would have to leave to have storytelling take place elsewhere. But the feathered immigrants were gone; so, a story, at least through the frozen times, could be told in the dead tree.

Somewhere in the direction inwhich the Rising Light rises, where vast and ice-free waters meet the land, a high rocky off shore island was the home of most cormorants, during the warm and cold periods. On and around this wave pounded isle these water skimmers hunted fish, nested, and rested upright together, in spite of the miseries the weather sent at them.

Sometime, but soon after many nonhumans went into the night to live, for some reason, only the Maker knows, their numbers increased. Their rock outcropped home became too crowded. The packed population was good for winter warmth as they huddled close to one another. But there was no room for nesting during the warm times. As the feathered combatants struggled to find a spot to occupy, many were forced off the island rock down into the splashing surf below.

Finally, in the beginning of one of the warm periods, some of the elder cormorants decided it would be best to have a meeting to discuss the packed problem.

Like a division of straight soldiers at close ranks, anchored to resist the sea winds, and with the elders perched at the highest points to preside over the feathered assembly, the talk began.

"We need more space," grunted a cormorant.

"It would even be better if there was less of us," whispered another.

"What are we to do?" muttered yet another while struggling to maintain a foothold.

Each was so focused that they had not notice that a gull had landed to eavesdrop among them. After listening for a few moments, the white air surfer brazenly interpreted. "Some of you should leave during the warmer times and nest elsewhere. Then, during the cold times, nestle here."

Surprised by the sudden harsh sound, some of the cormorants spread their wings to ready themselves to take flight. They quickly calmed when seeing the gull.

"Who are you, and what are doing here?" mumbled one of the elders.

"I am Gwylan. I am here resting," squawked the intruder.

"Your sounds are noisy and annoying," murmured the highest elder.

"And your sounds are barely audible. We are as the Maker of Nature made us." commented the gull.

"Yes, supposedly yes, "grunted many.

"Who shall go, and who shall stay?" quietly inquired the highest elder.

Gwylan looked up toward the speaker. "You and your peers can stay. Those who still nest can search for warm wind homes, returning to this place when the wind is cold.

Another elder silently spoke. "Those who go can't go farther into the Rising Light because the water that way is endless, and there are too many humans the opposite way toward the land."

The gull quickly responded to the elder's concern. "Have them fly to the left of the Rising Light until the Light is gone. Then turn left and keep going until pieces of water are seen on the land. The region is without too many human occupants. There they can choose nesting areas."

Each elder looked down on the aquatic flock and quietly spoke. "Listen to Gwylan. Find these warm period places to live. Go now while the Light is still rising."

One, then two, finally many, many voiceless cormorants leaped from the rock island, dove toward and darted across the choppy sea, gradually gaining attitude to follow the gull's instructions. The feathered throng was gone.

Alone with the elders and the breezes, Gwylan grinned and was pleased to have less competition in this area, at least, during the warm period.

A crow on shore witnessed the flight of the cormorants, and the lone gull on the offshore, rocky ledges. Springing from the protection of the trees, it fought the sea winds to reach the gull, to ask why.

"Now, Elegant, you know why many of the cormorants have come," continued Corvus.

"That cagey gull!" squawked the eagle. "Now, I have the competition! I wish I could get my claws on that grinning and cunning gull."

"You can't," said the storyteller. "That clever nonhuman resides far from here."

"I know," responded the disappointed eagle. "At least, now, it is that gull who is getting the cormorant's competition." The great bird spread its wings to allow the wind to lift it high above the dead tree. "Thank you, teller!" screeched the hooked bill glider as the air carried it away.

Corvus sat alone, feathers fluffed for warmth against the constant breezes, awaiting the coming of a deeper cold.

Brazen

by

Corvus Crow

Alone on his favorite branch of the dead tree, Corvus observed the sky filling itself with gentle falling flakes, some being absorbed by an iceless lake, and some whitening the land and everything on it. This would be his first frozen period home after being gone for a time to places to the right of the Rising Light.

The storyteller was suddenly surrounded on every limb by numerous, small feathered nonhumans, all chirping at once.

"Corvus! Corvus!" yelled the small feathered crowd. "It's Brazen! That thief chases us and takes our food!"

"Please, quiet down!" called the teller.

A temporary silence ensued.

"Good," continued the crow. "Now, what were you saying about that Jay? Please, speak one at a time."

"A few humans have placed food on the ground for us near their shelter," said one.

"Then as we eat, Brazen flies from the trees, forcing us to leave, and to wait elsewhere until that tyrant is finished," chirped another.

"Corvus, help us by speaking to that blue glutton?" speaking all together again.

"I am a teller, not a supervisor in this region," retorted the crow.

"But, you do have influence in this area," argued one more, small nonhuman

"I suppose I do," said the teller, proudly. "Well, I'll try to convince the Jay to eat and share with you." Actually, the crow gave in because he was tiring of debating with the feathered assembly.

"Oh, thank you," twittered the flock in unison. They then leaped away, causing a cloud of snow to form around the storyteller. The bunch quietly disappeared among the white trees.

Shaking the cold, white powder from himself, Corvus wondered how he was going to change the nature of the jay. The thought of Catus Cat came to mind. The crow spread his wings, and he too zigzagged to and through the frozen forest.

"Just where I thought I would find you, Catus!" cawed the teller.

The white cat bounced up from his favorite spot beneath the human made shelter, and stiffly stood looking about. "Corvus. I didn't see your approach," said the trembling cat.

"Nonhumans surprise me often too; because when I am alone, I am focused on my own thoughts," explained the storyteller.

"As I was!" squealed Catus. I too was focused, except my attention was on the feeding, feathered nonhumans. Now, however, you have frightened them away."

"Sorry, Catus. They will come back, and then you can chase them from their seed," responded the teller.

"I wish I could; however, eventhough my human caretakers have placed that food on the ground for those safe nonhumans, I am not allowed to run after them," the cat regretfully remarked.

"Too bad," replied the crow. "I was hoping you would just scare them a little for me."

"What! I mean, why, Corvus?" inquired Catus.

"Oh, I have my reasons," answered the storyteller.

"OK. Well, I suppose I could do some harassing when the humans are away," said the scheming cat. "Wait! Brazen Jay scatters those feathered feeders everyday. Why should I startle that dining crowd."

Because you are much larger and furred, and that means you are better at dispersing a feathered collection," the teller quickly answered.

"Yes, I am," replied the cat with head held high.

"Will you do it?" asked Corvus.

"Yes, when the humans are not around," responded Catus.

"Good. Thank you. I will leave now," cawed the crow.

The cat watched the storyteller take flight, and vanish among the winter trees.

Later, at his favorite tree, on his favorite branch, chirping chatter suddenly surrounded the teller.

"What is now?" asked the storyteller.

"Corvus, you don't have to speak to Brazen," cheeped one.

"Why is that?" questioned the crow.

"Brazen saved us from Catus," said another.

"How?" the teller inquired again.

"That unsafe, furred nonhuman began coming after us. Brazen flew out of nowhere, and darted at the cat many times. We have never seen Catus run away so fast," twittered yet another.

"Poor cat," mumbled Corvus.

"Brazen is our protector. If he wishes to eat without company, we'll gladly wait until he leaves," they all whistled at once.

"Sounds good," commented the storyteller.

As quickly as they came, the feathered group gave a quick good by, and winged away.

Staring across the cold lake, Corvus thought it would be proper to go and look for the cat, and apologize. He lifted his wings and was gone.

Herodias Heron

by

Corvus

Corvus fluffed his feathers for more warmth as he stared at a calm and slowly thawing lake under an overcast sky. Soon the feathered floaters and waders would return to this region. This had been his first winter home after having been gone a few seasons to a place to the right of the Rising Light.

There, there are human made lights that help ease any long winter grayness. A light pole had been his favorite storytelling perch. An old hollow riverbank willow had been his nightly and foul weather shelter.

He had become concerned about the possibility of too much human encroachment upon his northern home. So he returned to see for himself. His fears were unfounded. Human expansion at his home area was slow. But what of the nonhumans he had left behind to the right of the Rising Light? Are those nonhumans who were unable to live near humans safe from continuous human spreading? Probably not.

Now, back at his northern home, a white, frozen lake helps in piercing the long darkness of the cold period. His favorite storytelling perch is the openness of a dead, lake, shore tree, shared with cormorants during the warm times. His shelter is a nearby cedar.

"Corvus! Please, tell me a story!"

His thoughts suddenly disturbed, the startled teller took a deep breath, nervously shook his feathers, and turned toward the sneaky and loud intruder. It was Gnawen Chipmunk. "Are you finished with your winter naps?" asked the storyteller.

"No," answered the chipmunk. I am awake just long enough to eat some of my stored food and, maybe, hear a story from you. Then I'll take one more nap."

The teller once more stared toward the lake to focus on a story.

Far to the right of the Rising Light there is a network of three main rivers with banks that are lushly lined with different kinds of deciduous trees during the warm times. Back, maybe just after many nonhumans went into the night to live, and before the coming of many humans to that area, parts of the rivers would form ponds behind natural made blockages.

In the middle river, at one of its ponds, were the floaters and waders, who created numerous sounds of quacking and honking, particularly the low croaking sound of Herodias Heron. This large wader proudly strutted along the shallow shoreline, trying to fish with the other noisy, feathered probers.

Often this long legged nonhuman would look out toward the middle river lake, to deeper water, and stare with envy at the floaters there. Thinking aloud, he would say, "how nice it would be to be a floater, and to have access to all the fish in the center of the lake."

"Not a good idea," quacked a few, eavesdroppers nearby.

"You are not a floater," honked another seeing Herodias eyeing the lake.

Holding that long peak high, and angered by what was said, the heron argued, "I am feathered like you, and so, I should be able to float and fish too. In fact, I will prove it to you."

To the alarm of everyone, the great bird spread his large wings for lift.

"No! No! Herodias!" they all quacked and honked together.

The determined heron did not listen. All watched in disbelief as the giant wader flew up, then glided down, causing those who were already at the middle of the lake to quickly slid out of the way in all directions. Once on the water, the three toed nonhuman tried to float and paddle. However, there was no forward or even backward progress. Instead, all effort and energy was spent on wasteful splashing. Eventual sinking seemed possible.

The aquatic group close by immediately recognized the predicted problem, and hurriedly surrounded the frightened wader, and pushed him back to shore.

Happy to be on familiar ground, Herodias, stood up, shook off the moisture, and humbly said, "thank you." Embarrassed, the long legged strutter then left the company of the others to hunt alone. The great blue heron have since hunted solo; but has found great success in doing so.

A crow saw the clumsy wader in the center of the pond, and the rescue from a lakeside tree. The dark feathered nonhuman leaped to the air and winged to intercept the heron to ask why.

"Well, Gnawen," continued the storyteller. I have kept the story short, knowing that you desire to return to your nap."

"You are right," said the yawning chipmunk. "I will see you next time when I awake for a longer time."

"Everything will be awake then," commented the teller.

"That will be nice," answered Gnawen as he scampered down the dead tree.

Corvus resumed staring at the calm and waiting lake. His feathers waved in a mild breeze. This region was the place of his birth. He was glad to be home, in spite of the long, cold, and dark periods. Those are the obstacles that keep many humans from permanently placing themselves here. For now, the region is safe from too much human encroachment.

Gone

by

William R. Underwood

The persistent spring storms seemed to be finally finished. A stable summer would be welcomed. The water was mirror-like, so I decided to paddle to where I thought I saw the dark, feathered storyteller the year before.

I had recently purchased some acreage of shoreline property on this lake. The land would be only for seasonal use. For me the winters were too long and too cold for any extended stay. Being an urbanite, whose life has been spent surrounded by the racket of thousands of internal combustion engines, the quiet sounds of the area's birds, wind blown leaves and pine needles, pleasing noises, made the place a temporary relief. I also believed this was Corvus's home and his storytelling region.

There, laying half submerged, and outstretched from the shore, was what I remembered to be the naked tree, the teller's storytelling station. Marinus Cormorant and his same-feathered companions, along with Corvus, were gone.

I scanned all around the lake, looking to where they may have flown. Then, small waves began beating against my kayak. A strong wind was coming. It was now best to return to the property. Anyway, there was work to do there. I would search for the dark, feathered storyteller later. But where?

Later, at the property, while pulling the little boat ashore, I heard the flapping of wings in the cedar branches above me. It sounded like a large bird, like a hawk, or even an eagle. I stopped at what I was doing, and began to circle the tree, looking up among the limbs. It was an old cedar, therefore big enough to support something sizable. There, about half way up, I saw a black, feathered nonhuman, slightly smaller than a raven. One of its dark eyes peered back down to me. He seemed unconcerned of my presence. Beside him, on his hidden branch, were some smaller birds, wrens and chickadees. I was convinced it was the storyteller. My goodness! His home, shoreline tree, stood on my land! Corvus wasn't gone.